I Am the Cat

Also edited by Lee Bennett Hopkins

I Am the Cat

POEMS SELECTED BY LEE BENNETT HOPKINS

Illustrated by Linda Rochester Richards

HARCOURT BRACE JOVANOVICH
NEW YORK AND LONDON

LIBRARY OF CONGRESS CATALOGING IN PUBLICATION DATA
Main entry under title: I am the cat.
Contents: Life / Lee Bennett Hopkins—A Kitten / Eleanor
Farjeon—The kitten in the falling snow / James Kirkup—[etc.]
   1. Cats—Juvenile poetry. 2. Children's poetry, Ameri-
can. 3. Children's   poetry,   English. [1. Cats—Poetry.
2. American   poetry—Collections. 3. English   poetry—
Collections]   I. Hopkins, Lee Bennett.   II. Richards, Linda
Rochester.
PS595.C38I2   811'.008'036   81-2609
ISBN 0-15-237987-8   AACR2

Every effort has been made to trace the ownership of all
copyrighted material and to secure the necessary permissions
to reprint these selections. In the event of any question arising
as to the use of any material, the editor and the publisher,
while expressing regret for any inadvertent error, will be
happy to make the necessary correction in future printings.
   Thanks are due to the following for permission to reprint the
copyrighted materials listed below:

THOMAS Y. CROWELL, PUBLISHERS, for "The Kittens" from *My
Cat Has Eyes of Sapphire Blue* by Aileen Fisher. Copyright ©
1973 by Aileen Fisher.
CURTIS BROWN, LTD., for "Life" and "Cat's Kit" by Lee Bennett
Hopkins. Copyright © 1981 by Lee Bennett Hopkins.
FABER AND FABER LIMITED for "The Naming of Cats" from *Old
Possum's Book of Practical Cats* by T. S. Eliot.
FARRAR, STRAUS & GIROUX, INC., for "Cat" from *Small Poems*
by Valerie Worth. Poems copyright © 1972 by Valerie Worth;
and for "Tom" from *Still More Small Poems* by Valerie Worth.
Poems copyright © 1976, 1977, 1978 by Valerie Worth.
FOUR WINDS PRESS, A DIVISION OF SCHOLASTIC MAGAZINES, INC.,
for "Cat" from *Country Cat, City Cat* by David Kherdian.
Copyright © 1979 by David Kherdian and Nonny H. Kherdian;
and for "The Cat Lady" from *The Covered Bridge House and
Other Poems* by Kaye Starbird. Text copyright © 1979 by Kaye
Starbird Jennison.
HARCOURT BRACE JOVANOVICH, INC., for "The Naming of Cats"
from *Old Possum's Book of Practical Cats*, copyright, 1939, by
T. S. Eliot; renewed, 1967, by Esme Valerie Eliot.
JAMES KIRKUP for "The Kitten in the Falling Snow" and "The
Bird Fancier." Used by permission of the author who controls
all rights.

J. B. LIPPINCOTT, PUBLISHERS, for "A Kitten" from *Eleanor Far-
jeon's Poems for Children*. Originally published in *Over the
Garden Wall* by Eleanor Farjeon, copyright, 1933, 1961, by
Eleanor Farjeon.
LITTLE, BROWN AND COMPANY for "Cat & the Weather" from
New & Selected Things Taking Place by May Swenson.
Copyright © 1963 by May Swenson. By permission of Little,
Brown and Company in association with the Atlantic Monthly
Press.
MACMILLAN, LONDON AND BASINGSTOKE, for "Cat" by Alan
Brownjohn from *Brownjohn's Beasts*; and for "The Prayer of
the Cat" from *Prayers from the Ark* by Rumer Godden.
MCINTOSH AND OTIS, INC., for "It Happens Once in a While"
from *A Crazy Flight and Other Poems* by Myra Cohn
Livingston. Copyright © 1969 by Myra Cohn Livingston.
JAMES N. MILLER for "Cat" by Mary Britton Miller.
NEW DIRECTIONS PUBLISHING CORPORATION for "Poem" from
Collected Earlier Poems by William Carlos Williams.
Copyright 1938 by New Directions Publishing Corporation.
HAROLD OBER ASSOCIATES for "Cats" from *The Children's Bells*
by Eleanor Farjeon. Copyright © 1957 by Eleanor Farjeon.
LOUIS PHILLIPS for "Cat on the Radiator." Used by permission
of the author who controls all rights.
SIMON & SCHUSTER, A DIVISION OF GULF & WESTERN CORPORA-
TION, for "A Cat" by John Gittings from *Miracles* edited by
Richard Lewis. Copyright © 1966 by Richard Lewis.
WILLIAM JAY SMITH for "Moon" from *Laughing Time*, pub-
lished by Atlantic-Little, Brown, 1955, copyright, ©, 1955 by
William Jay Smith.
VIKING PENGUIN INC. for "The Prayer of the Cat" from *Prayers
from the Ark* by Carmen Bernos de Gasztold, translated by
Rumer Godden. Copyright © Rumer Godden 1962.

For
Bobbye S. Goldstein
who purrs poetry to children

Contents

Introduction

Poets sing of everything.

In this book, you will meet poets
who have sung the praises of cats, depicting them in
a variety of action and moods—from the playful,
mischievous, sometimes angelic kittens to the older,
independent, contemplative cats.

Keeping cats as pets dates back at least
five thousand years. Throughout the centuries
poets from China, England, France, and rural and urban
America have been inspired to pay tribute to one of
the most popular pets the world has ever known.

Meet the poets and their songs in *I Am the Cat*.

Lee Bennett Hopkins
SCARBOROUGH, NEW YORK

Life
LEE BENNETT HOPKINS

Newborn kittens
stumbled slowly
toward
their mother.

Snuggling into
her
tired-warm belly

they
readied for
their first
Tuesday morning
banquet.

A Kitten

ELEANOR FARJEON

He's nothing much but fur
And two round eyes of blue,
He has a giant purr
And a midget mew.

He darts and pats the air,
He starts and cocks his ear,
When there is nothing there
For him to see and hear.

He runs around in rings,
But why we cannot tell;
With sideways leaps he springs
At things invisible—

Then half-way through a leap
His startled eyeballs close,
And he drops off to sleep
With one paw on his nose.

The Kitten in the Falling Snow

JAMES KIRKUP

The year-old kitten
has never seen snow,
fallen or falling, until now
this late winter afternoon.

He sits with wide eyes
at the firelit window, sees
white things falling
from black trees.

Are they petals, leaves or birds?
They cannot be the cabbage whites
he batted briefly with his paws,
or the puffball seeds in summer grass.

They make no sound, they have no wings
and yet they can whirl and fly around
until they swoop like swallows, and
disappear into the ground.

"Where do they go?" he questions,
with eyes ablaze, following their flight
into black stone. So I put him
out into the yard, to make their acquaintance.

He has to look up at them: when one
blanches his coral nose, he sneezes,
and flicks a few from his whiskers, from
his sharpened ear, that picks up silences.

He catches one on a curled-up paw
and licks it quickly, before
its strange milk fades, then sniffs its ghost,
a wetness, while his black coat

shivers with stars of flickering frost.
—And with something else that makes his thin
tail swish, his fur stand on end!
Then he suddenly scoots in

and sits again with wide eyes
at the firelit window, sees
white things falling
from black trees.

The Kittens

AILEEN FISHER

How limp they lie
all curled together,
as listless as
the August weather,
entwined in most
endearing poses
of arms and legs
and necks and noses . . .

It's hard to think
that on awaking
they'll be so fired
with mischief-making.

The Prayer of the Cat
CARMEN BERNOS DE GASZTOLD

Lord,
I am the cat.
It is not, exactly, that I have something to ask of You!
No—
I ask nothing of anyone—
but,
if You have by some chance, in some celestial barn,
a little white mouse,
or a saucer of milk,
I know someone who would relish them.
Wouldn't You like someday
to put a curse on the whole race of dogs?
If so I should say,

Amen

Cat

MARY BRITTON MILLER

The black cat yawns,
Opens her jaws,
Stretches her legs,
And shows her claws.

Then she gets up
And stands on four
Long stiff legs
And yawns some more.

She shows her sharp teeth,
She stretches her lip,
Her slice of a tongue
Turns up at the tip.

Lifting herself
On her delicate toes,
She arches her back
As high as it goes.

She lets herself down
With particular care,
And pads away
With her tail in the air.

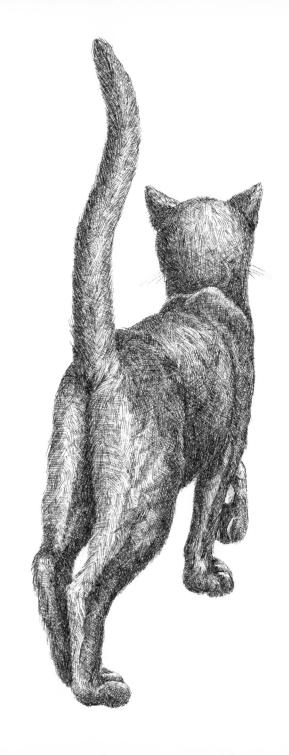

Cat's Kit
LEE BENNETT HOPKINS

Needle-like claws
Thimbled paws
Soft, silky, cushioney toes—

A
Siamese seamstress
wherever
        she
           goes.

Cat

ALAN BROWNJOHN

Sometimes I am an unseen
marmalade cat, the friendliest colour,
making off through a window without permission,
pacing along a broken-glass wall to the
   greenhouse,
jumping down with a soft, four-pawed thump,
finding two inches open of the creaking door
with the loose brass handle,
slipping impossibly in,
flattening my fur at the hush and touch of
   the sudden warm air,
avoiding the tiled gutter of slow green water,
skirting the potted nests of tetchy cactuses,
and sitting with my tail flicked
skilfully underneath me, to sniff
the azaleas   the azaleas   the azaleas.

Poem
WILLIAM CARLOS WILLIAMS

As the cat
climbed over
the top of

the jamcloset
first the right
forefoot

carefully
then the hind
stepped down

into the pit of
the empty
flowerpot

Chinese Proverb
ANONYMOUS

A lame cat
is better than a swift horse
when rats infest
the palace.

Cat & the Weather

MAY SWENSON

Cat takes a look at the weather.
Snow.
Puts a paw on the sill.
His perch is piled, is a pillow.

Shape of his pad appears.
Will it dig? No.
Not like sand.
Like his fur almost.

But licked, not liked.
Too cold.
Insects are flying, fainting down.
He'll try

to bat one against the pane.
They have no body and no buzz.
And now his feet are wet;
it's a puzzle.

Shakes each leg,
then shakes his skin
to get the white flies off.
Looks for his tail,

tells it to come on in
by the radiator.
World's turned queer
somehow. All white,

no smell. Well, here
inside it's still familiar.
He'll go to sleep until
it puts itself right.

Cat
VALERIE WORTH

The spotted cat hops
Up to a white radiator-cover
As warm as summer, and there,

Between pots of green leaves growing,
By a window of cold panes showing
Silver of snow thin across the grass,

She settles slight neat muscles
Smoothly down within
Her comfortable fur,

Slips in the ends, front paws,
Tail, until she is readied,
Arranged, shaped for sleep.

Cat on the Radiator
LOUIS PHILLIPS

Steam from its ears
Is truly steam.
The cat of the farmer
Dreams
To be warmer,
Her paws firmer,
Claws and fur,
The heat goes round,
Round
In a purr.
Radiator & cat,
It is difficult to be
Warmer
Than that.

The Naming of Cats

T. S. ELIOT

The Naming of Cats is a difficult matter,
  It isn't just one of your holiday games;
You may think at first I'm as mad as a hatter
When I tell you, a cat must have THREE DIFFERENT NAMES.
First of all, there's the name that the family use daily,
  Such as Peter, Augustus, Alonzo or James,
Such as Victor or Jonathan, George or Bill Bailey—
  All of them sensible everyday names.
There are fancier names if you think they sound sweeter,
  Some for the gentlemen, some for the dames:
Such as Plato, Admetus, Electra, Demeter—
  But all them sensible everyday names.
But I tell you, a cat needs a name that's particular,
  A name that's peculiar, and more dignified,
Else how can he keep up his tail perpendicular,
  Or spread out his whiskers, or cherish his pride?
Of names of this kind, I can give you a quorum,
  Such as Munkustrap, Quaxo, or Coricopat,
Such as Bombalurina, or else Jellylorum—
  Names that never belong to more than one cat.
But above and beyond there's still one name left over,
  And that is the name that you never will guess;
The name that no human research can discover—
  But THE CAT HIMSELF KNOWS, and will never confess.
When you notice a cat in profound meditation,
  The reason, I tell you, is always the same:
His mind is engaged in a rapt contemplation
  Of the thought, of the thought, of the thought of his name:
    His ineffable effable
    Effanineffable
Deep and inscrutable singular Name.

Moon

WILLIAM JAY SMITH

I have a white cat whose name is Moon;
He eats catfish from a wooden spoon,
And sleeps till five each afternoon.

Moon goes out when the moon is bright
And sycamore trees are spotted white
To sit and stare in the dead of night.

Beyond still water cries a loon,
Through mulberry leaves peers a wild baboon
And in Moon's eyes I see the moon.

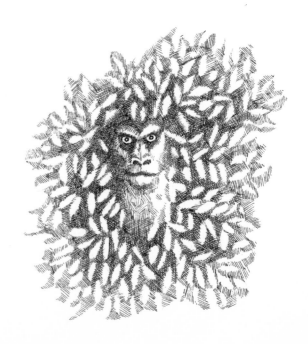

The Cat Lady

KAYE STARBIRD

Miss Flynn has over thirty cats.
At first she had two kittens,
A girl and boy
For fun and joy
Named Sport and Millie Mittens.

That April, Sport
And Mitt (for short)
Had babies: Scare and Lapkins,
Both born in style
Upon a pile
Of newly laundered napkins.

Then Lap and Scare
Became a pair
(Since girl cats mate with brothers)
Producing Puff
And Flounce and Fluff
And Blink and Moon and others.

And when *that* batch
Played mix-and-match
Cats crowded every nook,
And one named Hum
Kept peering from
Miss Flynn's best pocketbook.

And since their owner loves them all
And treats her home as theirs,
We're glad Miss Flynn
Did not begin
With two baboons or bears.

A Cat

JOHN GITTINGS
(at age 8)

Silently licking his gold-white paw,
Oh gorgeous Celestino, for
God made lovely things, yet
Our lovely cat surpasses them all;
The gold, the iron, the waterfall,
The nut, the peach, apple, granite
Are lovely things to look at, yet,
Our lovely cat surpasses them all.

It Happens Once in a While

MYRA COHN LIVINGSTON

Uncle Tiger just went out under the tree
   to get some sun.
He must have been tired. Sometimes,
   he gets that way.
He just stretched out with his long
   yellow paws quiet,
Half shutting his green eyes,
And then along came this silly,
   scolding old jay
And swooped down from the skies.
(You should have heard the riot!)
Uncle Tiger jumping up and biting
   that bright blue jay
And tearing off his feathers,
   one by one,
And, proud as can be,
Brings the jay to me.

It happens, once in a while.

The Bird Fancier

JAMES KIRKUP

Up to his shoulders
In grasses coarse as silk,
The white cat with the yellow eyes
Sits with his paws together,
Tall as a quart of milk.

He hardly moves his head
To touch with neat nose
What his wary whiskers tell him
Is here a weed
And here a rose.

His sleepy eyes are wild with birds.
Every sparrow, thrush, and wren
Widens their furred horizons;
Then their flying song
Narrows them again.

Tom

VALERIE WORTH

Old Tom
Comes along
The room
In steps
Laid down
Like cards,
Slow-paced
But firm,
All former
Temptations
Too humdrum
To turn
Him from
His goal:
His bowl.

The Cat
W. H. DAVIES

Within that porch, across the way,
I see two naked eyes this night;
Two eyes that neither shut nor blink,
Searching my face with a green light.

But cats to me are strange, so strange—
I cannot sleep if one is near;
And though I'm sure I see those eyes,
I'm not so sure a body's there!

Cats

ELEANOR FARJEON

Cats sleep
Anywhere,
Any table,
Any chair,
Top of piano,
Window-ledge,
In the middle,
On the edge,
Open drawer,
Empty shoe,
Anybody's
Lap will do,
Fitted in a
Cardboard box,
In the cupboard
With your frocks—
Anywhere!
They don't care!
Cats sleep
Anywhere.

Cat

DAVID KHERDIAN

The yellow bedspread
he sleeps upon
is slowly changing
to the gentle quiet
gold of his breath.

Cat of Cats
WILLIAM BRIGHTY RANDS

I am the Cat of Cats. I am
    The everlasting cat!
Cunning, and old, and sleek as jam,
    The everlasting cat!
I hunt the vermin in the night—
    The everlasting cat!
For I see best without the light—
    The everlasting cat!

Index

OF AUTHORS,
TITLES, AND
FIRST LINES